10.95

12

Marceau
Bonappétit

Marceau
Bonappétit

by Fanny Joly-Berbesson and
Dr. Brigitte Boucher

illustrated by Agnès Mathieu

 Carolrhoda Books, Inc./Minneapolis

Marceau Bonappétit is a young French mouse who can't wait to be on his own. Today is Friday, and Marceau's parents have decided to spend the weekend at Aunt Madeleine's house.

Marceau waves cheerfully as his parents go.

"Aren't you worried about leaving Marceau?" Marceau's dad asks.

"No, it's all arranged. He'll have his meals at friends' houses," answers Marceau's mom.

That evening, Marceau goes to the Hubbubs' for dinner. What an uproar at their house! Marceau rings the bell and waits. He rings again, but no one hears. Marceau taps, raps, and beats on the door. Oh, no! All his pounding has broken the window.

Marceau would like to apologize, but no one pays any attention to him. Mr. Hubbub is watching television, and Mrs. Hubbub is using the mixer. Big brother is listening to the radio, little sister is playing the xylophone, and big sister is on the telephone.

There is so much commotion during dinner that Marceau doesn't even notice the dishes passing right under his nose. When dinner is over, he hasn't eaten a thing.

That night, lying in his comfortable bed, Marceau has trouble falling asleep. His ears are ringing, and his head is pounding. He needs to get some sleep because tomorrow is Saturday, which is a school day in France.

Marceau is sound asleep when Albertine, his neighbor, arrives to walk to school with him. Marceau was so exhausted he slept through his alarm. He scrambles to get ready and rushes out the door. No time for breakfast this morning!

By eleven o'clock, Marceau is starving. He dreams of the breakfast his mom usually makes him: hot chocolate, French bread with jam, a boiled egg, some cheese, orange juice, and cereal with milk and fruit.

At noon, Marceau is as hungry as a wolf. He runs to the Gobble-alls', where he is expected for lunch. Mrs. Gobbleall has just come home with her shopping carts crammed with food. There are dozens of brightly colored boxes, bags, packets, bottles, and cartons, like the ones you see in commercials.

Marceau is getting hungrier and hungrier. Suddenly, everything around him starts to spin. He cries out, "I'm *so* hungry! I'm *too* hungry! I haven't eaten anything since yesterday at noon!"

And he falls on the floor in a faint.

When Marceau comes around, the Gobblealls are leaning over
him. He devours everything they offer him: green drinks,
greasy chips, rubbery cheese, and strange artificial desserts.

"Goodbye, and thanks very much!" says Marceau as he leaves
the Gobblealls'. "I love the things you eat here. I wish my mom
would buy them for me more often."

Marceau decides to stay home that afternoon. He really feels very odd. He keeps yawning, and his stomach hurts. One minute he wants to go to sleep. The next minute he feels sick. Mrs. Gobbleall stops by to make sure he's all right.

AT THE DREARYS'

That evening, Marceau feels uneasy as he goes into the Drearys' big, gray dining room.

"You're late, my boy," Mr. Dreary greets him sternly.

At the table, the Drearys don't speak at all.

"Um...it wasn't very nice out today, was it?" Marceau says, trying to be pleasant.

"No speaking at the table, Marceau," says Mrs. Dreary.

All through dinner, Clementine watches Marceau without saying a word.

"Why bother eating together if you can't even talk to each other?" Marceau wonders. The silent meal drags on, and Marceau begins to feel very sleepy.

"MARCEAU BONAPPÉTIT!"

Mr. Dreary's gruff voice wakes Marceau with a start. The horrible dinner is over. What a relief!

On Sunday morning, Marceau has almost finished his favorite breakfast when the telephone rings.

"Hello, Marceau? It's Suzy! Suzy Stuffer. It's noon. Have you forgotten about us? The whole family is here, and we're expecting you for lunch."

AT THE STUFFERS'

Marceau is dazed by the sight of all the dishes spread out on the Stuffers' dining room table.

"I hope you're really hungry!" says big Mrs. Stuffer, hugging little Marceau.

"Here at the Stuffers', we always finish everything on our plates," Suzy's mom declares proudly as she serves Marceau a giant helping of casserole.

"But we've already had soup and melon and snails and fish!" Marceau protests.

After the casserole, salad, cheese, cake, ice cream, and fruit, Marceau is sick of food. He would so much rather have played with Suzy and her cousins than have spent two hours eating.

What an afternoon! Marceau collapses on the couch. He doesn't even have the energy to play.

"I was so happy to see my parents leave. Now I just wish they'd come home."

At eight o'clock, there's a knock at the door.

"Dad, Mom!" cries Marceau. "Is that you?"

"No, Marceau. It's Coco, Coco Norbread-Norwater! We're expecting you for dinner at our house."

"You don't look well, Marceau," Mrs. Norbread-Norwater says anxiously.

"I think I'm a little bit ill," mumbles Marceau. "I'd just like a piece of bread and a big glass of water for dinner."

"Bread? We never eat bread! We don't want to get fat!" exclaims Mrs. Norbread-Norwater, putting out her cigarette.

"And we drink as little water as possible so we won't get bloated," adds Mr. Norbread-Norwater.

"No bread and no water, what a weird idea! Maybe that's why Coco always has a stomachache. And everyone knows smoking is worse than anything for your health," Marceau thinks to himself.

Suddenly, there's a knock at the door. It's Marceau's mom and dad!

MARCEAU'S PARENTS RETURN

On the way home, Marceau tells his parents all about his bizarre weekend, and he finishes by saying, "I was happy that you were going away, but then I couldn't wait for you to come home."

Marceau's appetite returns while his mom and dad make dinner.
His dad tells him, "Aunt Madeleine was sorry not to see you.
Why don't you write her a letter tonight?"

Dear Aunt Madeleine,

I was so sorry that I didn't come visit you this weekend. Please invite me to your house next weekend. I'll eat a loaf of bread and drink a bottle of water every day, and I won't eat anything artificial, okay? You won't make me finish everything on my plate or scold me if I talk at the table, will you?

We'll have delicious breakfasts without rushing or watching T.V., and without a lot of noise. Oh, it will be just great!

Kisses on both your cheeks and your moustache....

Your little mousie,
Marceau Bonappétit

Translated from the French by Amy Gelman.

This edition first published 1989 by Carolrhoda Books, Inc.
Original edition copyright © 1984 by Éditions du Centurion,
Paris, France, under the title MARCEAU BONAPPÉTIT.
This English translation copyright © 1989 by Carolrhoda
Books, Inc.
All rights reserved.

Library of Congress Cataloging-in-Publication Data

Joly-Berbesson, Fanny.
   [Marceau Bonappétit. English]
   Marceau Bonappétit / text by Fanny Joly-Berbesson and Brigitte
Boucher; illustrations by Agnès Mathieu.
       p.   cm.
   Summary: While his parents are away for the weekend, Mar-
ceau, a young mouse, discovers many new ways of eating when
he visits homes of five different friends.
   Translation of: Marceau Bonappétit.
   ISBN 0-87614-369-9
   [l. Eating customs — Fiction. 2. Mice — Fiction.] I. Boucher,
Brigitte. II. Mathieu, Agnès, Ill. III. Title
PZ7.J6625Mar   1989
[E] — dc19   88-36425
                                                  CIP
                                                  AC

Manufactured in the United States of America.

1 2 3 4 5 6 7 8 9 10 99 98 97 96 95 94 93 92 91 90 89